Dear Parents,

Welcome to the Scholastic Reader series. We have taken over 80 years of experience with teachers, parents, and children and put it into a program that is designed to match your child's interests and skills.

Level 1—Short sentences and stories made up of words kids can sound out using their phonics skills and words that are important to remember.

Level 2—Longer sentences and stories with words kids need to know and new "big" words that they will want to know.

Level 3—From sentences to paragraphs to longer stories, these books have large "chunks" of texts and are made up of a rich vocabulary.

Level 4—First chapter books with more words and fewer pictures.

It is important that children learn to read well enough to succeed in school and beyond. Here are ideas for reading this book with your child:

- Look at the book together. Encourage your child to read the title and make a prediction about the story.
- Read the book together. Encourage your child to sound out words when appropriate. When your child struggles, you can help by providing the word.
- Encourage your child to retell the story. This is a great way to check for comprehension.
- Have your child take the fluency test on the last page to check progress.

Scholastic Readers are designed to support your child's efforts to learn how to read at every age and every stage. Enjoy helping your child learn to read and love to read.

> **—Francie Alexander**
> Chief Education Officer
> Scholastic Education

Copyright © 1996 by Nancy Hall, Inc.
Fluency activities copyright © 2003 Scholastic Inc.

All rights reserved. Published by Scholastic Inc.
SCHOLASTIC, CARTWHEEL BOOKS, and associated logos are trademarks
and/or registered trademarks of Scholastic Inc.

Library of Congress Cataloging-in-Publication Data is available.

ISBN 0-439-59427-8

10 9 8 7 6 5 4 3 2   05 06 07
Printed in the U.S.A.   23
First printing, August 1996

AT THE CARNIVAL

by Kirsten Hall
Illustrated by Laura Rader

Scholastic Reader — Level 1

Cartwheel
B·O·O·K·S ®

SCHOLASTIC INC.
New York Toronto London Auckland Sydney
Mexico City New Delhi Hong Kong Buenos Aires

A carnival!

Stay by my side.

Stay by my side

for every ride!

A rocket ship!

A bumper car!

Stay by my side, and don't go far!

A water slide!

A water slide!

My favorite ride!

A merry-go-round!

Around and around...

I'm lost!

I'm lost!

And now I'm found!

Around and around we ride
and ride.

Now, don't go far! Stay by my side!

Rebus Words

Can you recognize these words from the story?

+ nival = ?

+ et = ?

r + + d = ?

Opposites

Opposites are words that mean something completely different.

For each word on the left point to its opposite on the right.

go   far

lost   up

near   found

down   stop

Carnival!

Point to five things that are wrong at this carnival.

Rhyme Time

Look at the words and pictures in each row. Point to the picture that rhymes with each word.

far

by

now

pocket

So Many Rides

Which is your favorite carnival ride?

Does it go fast or slow?

Does it go up and down?

Does it go around and around?

Why do you like it?

Answers

(Rebus Words)

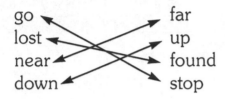 + nival = carnival

![rock] + et = rocket

r + 👁 + d = ride

(Opposites)

go   far
lost   up
near   found
down   stop

(Carnival!)

These things are wrong:

(Rhyme Time)

far   ![car]   (car)

by   👁   (eye)

now   🐄   (cow)

pocket ![rocket] (rocket)

(So Many Rides)

Answers will vary.